Little Though I Be

story and pictures by
JOSEPH LOW

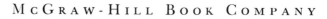

McGraw-Hill Book Company

New York • St. Louis • San Francisco • Düsseldorf • Johannesburg

Kuala Lumpur • London • Mexico • Montreal • New Delhi • Panama

Rio de Janeiro • Singapore • Sydney • Toronto

Little Though I Be

1234567 RABP 789876

Library of Congress Cataloging in Publication Data

Low, Joseph, date.
  Little Though I Be.

  SUMMARY: Convinced that his father favors his two taller brothers, a little boy turns to his animal friends for help in gaining his father's approval.

  [1. Fathers and sons—Fiction] 1. Title.
PZ7.L9598LI   [E]   75-42195
ISBN: 0-07-038842-3
ISBN: 0-07-038843-1 lib. bdg.

Well now, there was once a boy named Timothy. But everyone called him Tim, for he was a short boy, shorter by far than his two tall brothers, Ted and Tad.

This troubled him sorely, not because he begrudged them their long legs and strong backs, but because their father favored his two big sons.

The father would smile as he watched Ted and Tad, each doing the work of three, and with no sweat or strain about it. When there would be visitors, the father, without thinking, would boast: "Sure there's no man alive has two such great sons as mine!"— forgetting entirely his third, small Tim.

Tim would lie in his bed at night and think, "Why can't he see, as I do, that though I'm short of leg, I'm long in wit? Little though I be, yet I've twice the brains of those great fellows, and a sharper eye as well."

It got so that Tim went less and less to work in the fields, and spent more and more time in the barn and in the woods. For he had made a wonderful discovery: he could talk to the birds and beasts and could understand all they said. He had given them all secret names, so he might call them when he wanted them.

Like once when he felt the need of a bit of chat to
cheer him up, he called out:

> *"House-walk, let us talk;*
>
> *Let us, I say."*

And there, down the leafy path of the woods, crept
the turtle, for all the world like a walking house,
swaying as he came. And they had a fine, long chat.

But as Tim spent more and more time with the beasts and birds, he had less and less to give to his chores, and he neglected them badly without really thinking about it. But his father thought about it, and he got angrier and angrier. Finally one day his wrath poured up from his heart and out of his mouth in a stream of hot words.

"What a useless baggage you are, Tim! Little you do for what you get, and we working to feed, clothe and shelter you. Sure, there's days and nights, too, when I wonder are you any son of mine at all. Between books, birds, and beasts, you're a waste to the family. Do you plough or plant or harvest? Do you cut or carry wood? While we work, you dream! Sooner than food from the field, I'd expect you might bring through that door some golden bird, and it singing some magic tune. It'd be like you, sure, but I'll not hold my breath till the great day comes!" And he turned aside and stamped upstairs to his bed.

While he sat sadly by the hearth, Tim heard his dad's boots hit the floor above when he threw them down. As the fire burned low, his heart grew small and tight; but he kept on thinking, and just as the last spark died, it came to him: "There's no hope of matching those two here at home. Maybe beyond the hills lie things I can do or find, better than they ever dreamed of—if they dream at all—something wondrous to win my dad's good will again." And with that to comfort him, he fell asleep.

Waking early the next morning, before the rest
were even stirring in their beds, he slipped out of the
house. As he went, he spoke to each of his friends in
turn. All gave the promise to come at his call when he
might need them. And one gave more:

"You're a clever lad," said the crow, "and wit is the
key to many locks. Go see what lies over the hills.
Who knows what you'll find? And when you need one
of us, he'll be at your side the moment you call."

So Tim tightened his belt, turned to the west, and
set off for the hills.

Well, he climbed one hill and then another, and as he came to the top of the third, there lay a broad sea, so wide he could not see the further shore. "Now is the time," he thought, "and the first time, too." And he sang out:

"*Gallop, bring shallop;*
Bring shallop, I say."

In those days, shallop was the name for a small sailboat, and since there was a fine breeze blowing in the right direction, it was just what he needed.

Quick as a wink, there came his friend the horse, pulling a fine shallop along the shore by means of a rope in his teeth.

"Thank you, dear friend," said Tim. "I must be off and away, but I will be back, you may be sure." And he leaped from bank to boat.

But when he went to set the sail, he could not find the rope that would pull it up. So he called out:

"Long-tail, set the sail;

Set it, I say."

Quick as a wink, there was the little gray mouse, scurrying up the mast to get the rope. As he pulled it down, up went the sail, and the boat began to move.

"Thank you, dear friend," said Tim. "I must be off now, but I will be back, with maybe a bird in my hand and joy in my heart." And he jumped to the steering oar, for the shallop had begun to fly over the waves like the fine skimming boat she was.

In no time at all, the distant shore appeared and the wind dropped down to a soft breeze, just enough to press the boat against the slope of the beach so Tim could step ashore without so much as wetting his boots.

He looked about at the new land where he found himself, and it was strange indeed: nothing like the old farm and fields he knew so well. There were cherries big as pumpkins, pumpkins in the tree tops, and fish flying in and out among them all.

"Marvelous," thought Tim, "but I've work to do and no time for staring. I must get on with it or never a golden bird I'll see." So he looked about till he found a road going off into the hills. He set off briskly, but he hadn't got far when he found his way blocked by a great wall and a gate so high he could never reach the latch, though he could see it plainly enough.

"What my hand cannot, my voice may do," said
Tim to himself, and he called out:

> *"Rat-catch, lift the latch;*
> *Lift it, I say."*

Quick as a wink, there was the cat, nimble and clever,
scampering up the gate and taking the latch string in
her teeth for a good, strong pull, to let the gate swing
wide.

"Thank you, dear friend," said Tim. "I must be off
now, but I will be back with the bird in hand and a
smile in my heart." And he passed through the gate
and on up the road. As the hills got steeper, the air
grew colder, and Tim had to run to keep himself
warm.

All at once, he found his way blocked by a great pair of boots. "What's this?" asked Tim. "Such a great pair of boots! My brothers' big brogans could slip beneath the arch of them and never be seen."

And he looked a bit higher, and there he saw a great pair of britches above the boots, and a coat to match, above them, and far up in the air above all else, a huge bearded face scowling down.

"Well then," said Tim to himself, "since he's so big, I'll make myself small and just sneak 'round that left boot there, and go my way."

But when he made his move, the left boot moved, too, and blocked his way again. "So I'll try the right," said Tim, and he did, but with no more luck than the left allowed. Back and forth, side to side he went, for maybe a dozen tries in all. "This won't do," said Tim. "I'm getting nowhere at all, and time is running out."

Cupping his hands to his mouth, he yelled with all his might, "What is it you want, Great Boots, to take yourself out of my path?"

The giant's eyes flickered and his ears twitched, but no answer came down from the great mouth behind the wiry whiskers.

"Well," thought Tim, "big fellows are often slow of wit, but this one, I am sure, is holding back on purpose." And he called over his shoulder, in a quieter voice:

> *"Feather-beak, make him speak;*
> *Make him, I say."*

Quick as a wink, there was the wise old crow, perched on the giant's ear, cawing into it; but so far above him Tim couldn't hear what he said. Whatever it was, it did the job. The giant's eyes lighted up, his mouth began to move, and the crow flew down.

"Thank you, dear friend," said Tim. "You must be off, I know; but we'll meet at home: me with the bird in hand and a spring to my step."

The giant's mouth opened wide at last and out came his voice, surprisingly calm and reasonable. "I'll not let you pass," said he, "till you've brought fire to light that heap of logs. I've stood on this cold, high hill for twenty years and it's beginning to chill my bones."

"No problem there," thought Tim, "but I must be quick, for the wind blows hard and the cold is cutting through my own thin shirt." And he called out:

"Sun-crier, bring fire;
Bring fire, I say."

Quick as a wink, nothing happened, nor yet in the time of three winks; but in the time of four, the rooster came shooting through the air like a fiery rocket, with a bit of the sun in his claws. (It had taken the extra time to get there and back, for the sun is far, far away, you know.) He flew straight to the logs and set them crackling, red and smokey.

"Thanks, dear friend," said Tim. "I know you must be off now, and back to your lady hens. But we'll meet again, me with the golden bird in hand, and maybe a feather in my cap."

As the heat rose from the flames, the giant stooped to feel the good of it, his eyes glowing and his whiskers parted in a broad smile.

"Now then," said Tim, "just remember your promise and let me by, for I've far to go before my goal is won."

"Why, to be sure," said the giant in his gentle voice, "I'll do better than that." And he reached down and picked up Tim, ever so lightly, and without so much as moving one boot, he leaned far over the hills and set Tim down just outside the wall of a castle, perched high on the tallest peak of all.

"You are as kind as you are big," said Tim, "and I wish you comfort from the heat of your fire."

And he began to walk 'round the castle, looking for
a gate in the wall; but he could find none. He walked
near an hour and knew he'd been around it entirely
for, like the clever boy he was, he had marked the
ground before he started.

"Where you can't go through, go over," thought
Tim; and he sang out:

> *"Swiftly, lift me;*
> *Lift me, I say."*

Quick as a wink, the goose came whistling in on her
wide, white wings. Tim leaped on her back and off
they flew, over the walls, between the towers, till
they came to the tallest tower of all, where she set him
down, just at its door, which stood ajar.

"Thank you,
dear friend," said Tim.
"You must be off,
I know, and back to
the pond in the fold
of our hills;
but we'll meet again,
me with the
bird in hand and a
jump to my legs."
And he went through
the door and
into the tower.

And there he saw—guess what? A golden bird on a golden nest, glowing in the gloom.

But when he reached out to grab it, he banged his knuckles hard against a dome of glass which covered it and couldn't be budged.

As he sucked his fist to ease the pain, Tim saw a strange set of figures on the glass:

"Sure, I can read every book on my father's shelf," said Tim, "but this beats all, and I need help." So he called out, having taken his fist from his mouth:

"Wing fiddle, solve riddle;
Solve riddle, I say."

Quick as a wink, there was the cricket, striding back
and forth over the glass figures, studying them
carefully, now this way, now that.

And he looked at Tim, and he said, "This is deep indeed. It's going to take time."

"Take as much as you must, but no more, dear friend," said Tim, "for it's long since my breakfast and I'm feeling faint."

Then the cricket began to hum softly to himself, pacing from sign to sign and back again. It seemed hours to hungry Tim before, at last, he cried in his shrill, sharp voice: "Look you, now: take the sound as it comes from the signs and you'll have the meaning clear enough. That eye is for *I*; the M is for *am*; the red E is for *ready;* the 2 is for *to;* the bee is for *be;* the U and the R's make *yours.* Put them together and they say, 'I am ready to be yours.'"

As he spoke the last word, there was a loud *crack*! and a long tinkle as the glass dome shattered and fell in pieces to the floor, though none on Tim or on the cricket. "Now, my boy," said the cricket, "just reach out and take your prize."

"Thank you, dear friend," said Tim. "I know you must be off and back to the warm hearth of home; but I'm near the end of my task and before long you'll see me there, with this bird in hand and a welcome, I hope, from my dad."

So he did reach out, and he did grasp the nest and the bird on it; but still he was far from the old farm and the good word he longed to hear. "Once again," he said to himself, "and this the last time of all." And he raised his voice in the dark of the tower:

> *"Blue-back, carry me back;*
> *Carry me, I say.*
> *Saying, I sing,*
> *And singing I say,*
> *Carry me over the sea and away."*

Quick as a wink, there was the great heron, slanting down from the sky, to lift him and his treasure into the air. Fast and far they flew, over mountains and waves, down at last to their own green farm and small, white house.

"Thank you, dear friend," said Tim, "and my thanks to all the other lovely birds and beasts. Now my roaming is done. Here I am, home again, with the bird in hand and a droop to my eye, for I'm weary indeed from my travels." And he walked through the door and, without a word, handed the bird to his father.

Well, Tim's was not a bad father after all. It was just that, like so many of us, he saw best what he wanted most to see, and that had always been his two tall sons. But a golden bird is a golden bird, all the more so when it sits on a golden nest.

The father's eyes flew open and his mind began to whirl. He ran to the door and cried out, "Come running, you Ted and Tad! See what our Tim has brought!"

The two big ones were busy moving cattle from one
field to another. And how did they do it? They tossed
the cows from hand to hand, till all were munching in
the new green grass. Ted looked at Tad with a grin;
and Tad said to Ted, "Our dad must be getting soft,
surely, for what could small Tim bring in but some
mouse or sparrow he has tamed in the wood?"

But to humor the old man, they left cattle and
fields and went to the house, scorning the gates and
striding over the walls. Ducking their heads to get
through the door, they saw nothing till they
straightened up again. They looked first at their
Dad, then at Tim, and at last saw the shining bird on
its shining nest.

At that moment, the bird opened his beak and, having tried a few trills and runs, sang on in a clear, sweet voice which held them all enchanted. Only poor Tim was so weary he slipped in and out of sleep as the bird sang on.

As he slid to the floor, did he hear his Dad say to Ted and Tad, "Now then, me fine buckos, didn't I always tell you and all others this lad carried a great weight of brain above his shoulders. And isn't that the best muscle of them all?"

Did he, or didn't he?
What do you think?